VOIDEUSE

BY

KAISA SAARINEN

FERAL DOVE BOOKS
SEATTLE
2022

these pages conta

stage knives and safety needl

CONTENTS

Exonerate me

Let me be your little moon,
lunar beck, a dionean shipwreck.
Take me off your orbit soon -
I'll still dream your hands around my neck.

You must be sick of hearing me apologise
so exonerate me, take away my voice.
Make a noose for me, I'll follow through,
prayer-mute and powder-blue.

I'm so tired of negotiation. Give me easy absolution
cut off my tongue with the right hymns unsung
blacken my gaze blank eyes ablaze
a metal spoon would suffice

I want to be a sacrifice
a luminous violent lust -
grind me to planetary dust!

THERE WAS A WARNING

A white mist rises in the valley of electric wires.
My windchime mind cries out at every touch
a bright sound, a broken glass.
But I'm a dirty window.
Can you see anything through me –
anything at all? This fever
keeps dragging me under
the yellowed wallpaper
seeped with cigarette smoke.

I stopped playing with the ashes
only after their silvery soot buried me.
Breathing in and out
every day the same episode unfolds.
Give the TV a little kicking.

All there is to life
a dull knife that won't kill me quick
hanging overhead
with its own strange force field.

Pixels of snowfall ink black sludge
I want to be shocked by your touch.
You take this blood-heeled waltz
through the witching hour,
pull me closer like a smiling cat drags
roadkill through the door.

I'm not a lazy dancer, I'm
being strangled by a veil you can't see,
wedded to a lucid uncertainty.
The last chapter closes in
and I don't know the ending
but I feel it in my bones.
Won't you tell me the breaking order?
Your embrace fi lls me with a sincere dread.

Let me go limp in the machine arms
of a visionary angel looking at the mirror
incandescent with sorrow.

Let me be the vessel,
run through my pale blue veins
a thick prescription of revelations.

IMAGES OF CRUELTY

Last Tuesday, Terese had gone to get her nails done for the first time in months.

'I can tell you've been walking too much', the pedicurist had said. 'Too much dead skin on a young girl like you.'

'Who hasn't at this point?' she'd snapped in defense.

In her heart, though, she knew her walking habits were beyond the boundaries of normality. In the bitter cold of winter, she'd regularly completed two-hour walks down to Greenwich to see a man who treated her with utmost malice. The summer before, she'd discarded her crutches and forced herself to walk on fractured shins. Whenever someone offered to buy her an Uber, she naturally recoiled. They were not meant for her – hers was the domain of trains & buses & dirty soles.

She preferred men who never even asked, who didn't stop and think about how she moved her body to and from their apartments. It meant less pressure to come up with excuses. Women never let her get away with it so easily. Promise me you won't walk home this time, they would plead. It's so late. I don't like you taking the night bus, it's unsafe. Please let me get it for you if you can't pay. She frequently resorted to lying, saying she'd booked an Uber and slipping outside to turn half the street-corners of the city until she made it home. It was a point of pride.

Still, that evening, Terese accepted the Uber. Her date was ludicrously rich, a man she would only ever sleep with for the possibility of capital gain. Unlike in regular dating, there was no illusion of level ground. She had to at least try and claw her way up, even if she already knew the task was Sisyphean.

She got into a car with darkened windows and breathed in, out, in, made awkward small talk with the driver – Look at all the people packed into that pavilion, dancing like they're above it all – It seems they're filming a movie – Well that's no excuse. You a key worker too, Miss?

Unsurprisingly, the man turned out to be small. a lowercase daddy. The bookshelves in his cavernous living room were decorated by art auction catalogues and photographs of his children. Terese averted her eyes, straightening her navy sailor dress while he finished up an important phone call. She watched cubes of ice melt into her glass of diet coke, handed to her by a pretty eastern European maid.

'You're exactly Anthony's type', she had informed her in a dating app message that morning. 'Rare'.

They could have switched positions so easily. Terese imagined herself in the maid's collared little dress, spending her mornings looking up girls her boss might like to fuck online, her evenings handing out little drinks to them. How she would learn to view women as sets of attributes, ticking off things he found attractive. What was it about me? Should I thank you for the privilege? The maid was smiling at her, saccharine sweet. Terese wanted to enter a mirror.

She was alone with Anthony, now.

'You seem nervous', he said.

'I'm not used to this', she said, fidgeting with her hands on her lap.

'To meeting new people?'

'Yes.'

'Tell me about your studies.'

'I'm writing my dissertation about muzan-e.'

'What's that?'

'Art history. Images of cruelty.'

She had graduated two years before, with honours in pure mathematics.

'Like what?'

'Pregnant women strung up in fishermen's ropes and flayed alive. Innocent civilians beheaded on the street by bored samurai. That kind of thing.'

Anthony smiled beamingly. 'I'm into that.'

Do you realise you're the butt of their joke? She didn't ask, naturally. She smiled and played with her hair until his hands crept on her thighs. His fingers were shorter than hers.

When he kissed her, Terese tried to make herself feel grateful instead of recoiling. He is just making space for me in a world that is not mine.

'Can I hurt you now?' he asked. She nodded and followed him into another room.

'Take off your dress.' He was putting on a stern voice that did not suit his little body. She pulled the navy dress over her head.

'I like your corset.' He unlaced it to insert metal clamps on her nipples and her clitoris.

In pain, she watched him do three lines of coke. Terese liked thinking of her pain as a gift. Anthony was looking away, failing to fully receive any of it. Without audience, her eyes watered. It was simply a resistance test. She knew she could take it. She could take anything.

After she'd passed the probe, Anthony gave her some drugs, but they did nothing for her. It was extremely difficult for her to experience a high; taking pain was the most effective way she'd found to get endorphins into her bloodstream. She looked at Anthony's glazed eyes and knew he would be unable to have sex with her. Small mercies.

'Have you ever used a Sybian?' he asked.

She shook her head at the alien word. Smiling, he walked to a cupboard and pulled out a black suitcase.

'Open it for me, baby.'

Inside was a little sex machine, a saddle-mounted dildo. He handed her a remote control with two circular knobs. 'I want to see you come.'

I would never.

Terese turned the knobs to maximum intensity and remained very still, relishing the punishing grate of hard plastic against her insides.

'Good girl.' He was taking a video on his iPhone.

She could turn this into an endurance test, too. Some time passed – three or ten minutes, a small eternity.

'Do you feel close?'

'No.'

'I've never seen anyone use it this long', he said, frowning at her.

The machine was loud enough to drown her whimpers. She wondered which would come first, bleeding or blacking out. Anthony left her to her own devices, skulking out of the room.

She was convulsing electronically. She was brimming with spirits; she knew that when they started streaming down her cheeks. After she flicked the switch into the 'off' position, lightning bolts kept running up and down her spine, lashing between her shaky legs. In a triumphant feat of alchemy, she had neutralised the threat of excess pleasure by turning it into nothing, or something she had no name for.

On the cab ride back home, Terese rested her hot forehead against the window and looked up. It was not stargazing, because the sky had turned into a negative space, black as the ink of lecherous octopi. She knew it was not empty.

SPECTRAL ANGUISH

It is simple to become a ghost.
    Still bones,
    still heart.
Remains in solitude.
Wintry windows, pitch dark screens.

Good girls shall be seen not heard.
Good ghosts stay in forever waiting.
(I know that is not true)
(Nobody ever told me that
  and yet)
No destruction in my fingertips.

I always wanted to sing but
opened my mouth to be terror-struck.
How does a child like that ever learn to haunt?

(One day one bright blue day may come
of being exorcised by you my love)

A phantom pain in the larynx,
a fading light on the switchboard.
I will never make the call.

Park Hotel

Bare feet sink into the dusty depths of red carpet

unilluminated by cold sealight. All along this corridor of dirty windows

others sleep. Greeted by the moonlike glow of the ice machine, I kneel

make a frail vessel of my palms. Filled with dread for this thawing world

I dare not think of what waits beneath the frozen surface

The translucent spheres in my hands reveal nothing. Obscure eyes of the

anaesthetised

I press them against my cheeks, a wintry blush absent emotion.

I walk down every street of Reykjavik planting ice. Softly softly pleading

spare me

from the horrors of spring

The apple trees have bloomed early this year. Their pale petals cover the dry earth, and I can't avoid stepping on them as I walk through the yard. The crunch-crunch-crunch of flowers beneath my feet is nauseating. I try walking at a slower pace, but the mass of my body is always going to be too much for them to withhold. The air is crystallising in my lungs as I reach the door.

People have different thresholds for pain.

'It's white outside', you say, transfixed by the window, as I enter the room. You are sitting up on the bed in blue, back straight, shoulders lined up with perfect tension. 'Just like last February.'

'Last February, it was snow. This time it's apple flowers.'

'Oh.' Your voice is small and thoughtful. 'That's even nicer.'

The smile is there in the corners of your eyes, and that is enough. I brush my fingers over your wrist, catching your pulse. The rhythmic crush of flowers underfoot still lingers in my ears. After that bright sound, the beat of your heart is leaden.

'Your hand is burning', you wince, and I withdraw as swiftly as if I'd been brandished by hot coals myself.

Inspecting the thin layer of skin coating your wrist for scalds, I find its dull milky colour unchanged.

'It felt nice', you murmur.

'If you're not hurting then are you even human?' an ex-girlfriend once said to me. She had meant it rhetorically, but I'd felt at loss for an answer regardless. It was a nocturnal rooftop conversation, high and juvenile, not something to obsess over for years afterward; yet I have kept spinning it in endless circles ever since then.

The truth is that I have always been stricken by an absence of any strong emotion. When the doctor called to solemnly say you are not getting better, I was seized by the thought I should cry, but my body was too full of static. I had the stage directions laid out in front of me, but I couldn't follow them. I said thank you for letting me know and put the phone down and went dancing to fill my head with another kind of noise. When my friends found out, none of them spoke to me for weeks. I couldn't defend myself. I agreed – completely, ceaselessly, categorically – that there was something wrong with me. I pricked myself with pins, caressed my skin with graters, tried my hand at a knife, but I only managed to hurt my epidermis.

Resigned, I remained in that closed circuit (an ache that was mine and mine only, indivisible), caressing my boundaries with sharp instruments.

Within this small sterile room that has become your world, I know it is to protect myself from a greater, brighter pain; that of letting my outlines grow porous, allowing in sound and light. Realising that I'm one with a world that is always screaming and dying, how can I not feel sick? And, still, there are early-blooming apple trees in the hospital yard, the perfect angle of sunbeams on a stark white wall. The pain of both existing at the same time, being part of me at the same time, you dying and the earth being gently covered in a veil of white. I want to keep holding your hand, even when both of us flinch away.

GRASPING

Most things are shadows
of what
I hope I'll never know
These hands are shadow hands
Real hands would have strangled
something long ago

Certain poems scrape the ceiling
of their unholy observatory
pronouncing something forbidden
a transcendental joy

I gaze at the penumbra of revelations
a false light breaking through the sky
red valerian grows taller than the house

In a time of drought cover every mirror
when the songbirds have changed
the shape of your limbs is not important
for burying dead skin in charred leaves
there is no severed self.

Watch the dream of a bonfire
on your knees in wet black soil
only desire ascendant. Rise. Rise

in felled whitebirch solitude
without witness truth
of things slips away

Before winter
another winter
never meeting the golden world

Half forms in the mirror
the face, a sliver
through tr
auma
äumerei
epanation

A lens in my brain
shall give my own testimony
look at this
show me (who?)
how real
how real

SOURCE CODES

By inserting a secondary heart, [girl] renders into
[biological object] – alien in history class
body of indifferent nature. Her handwriting: the same as it ever was.

Sydämen kaksinkertaus muuntaa [tyttösen] joksikin
kemian tunnilla itseään tutkiva [objekti]
julmuuden luomiskertomus. Käsiala ei muutu

二重の心臓によって「少女」は変化し
歴史の授業中に自身を眺める「対象」
自然は無関心。手書は変わらない

DIVIDE ET IMPERA

For as long as I can remember, people have been telling me I look lost - on the street, in my own birthday parties, in fetish clubs. They say it kindly, with big eyes and mild concern in their voice. You seem lost, so how can I help you? I only wish they would stop assuming I want to be found. I love having no spatial awareness and floating just outside my body; I love it and it is terrifying. Terrifying when I float too far away and I'm not here anymore. When I am lost like that, no stranger can give me the directions back to where I need to be. Does that place even exist? The older I grow the more I doubt it, and the less it worries me.

'You look lost', a man shouts at me over the music. 'You OK?'. I nod, and he nods and shows mercy, disappearing down a darkened corridor. Sometimes the right to remain lost is only given after lengthy negotiations. Luckily, I am in a party full of people who are all too happy to focus only on themselves.

This night is syrupy, suffocating, and I'm struggling to keep my head above the surface. The waters aren't gentle. At the edges of my consciousness, a static buzzes like a chainsaw, grinding violently. I'm not going to listen to it. I'm not going to die. Besides, this house is already a little hell, so hot and humid that everyone needs to keep moving just to stop spores from growing on their clothes, on their skin - I imagine little colonies of black mould covering my arm and shudder, drowning the thought into a kiss. My target is chosen by pure proximity, or it could be fate. A tattooed man with close-cut hair, his mouth bitter and stale. He laps at my tongue like a big cat licking a saucer. I squeeze my eyes shut and try to stay very still.

'Why don't you kiss me like you mean it', he says. I open my mouth a little wider. It's disgusting.

'What's your name?' he asks, and I say the first thing that pops into my head. 'Celia.' I don't want to know a single one of his biographical details, so I lean closer to his ear and whisper: 'Do you want to fuck me?' in a crude change of tactics. He stumbles on his feet before nodding. I kiss the tattoo covering his neck, a red orchid with a blue dove in its mouth. I won't look at his face, because only his stranger-ness can kill the familiarity of my dread.

The bathroom tiles are swirling in blue, a cold comfort against my knees. I unbuckle his belt without glancing up, take him into my mouth, and it's like the kiss, comfortingly unpleasant. The man is too high. I work him for a while before giving up.

'I don't think it's going to happen', I say and get back on my feet.

'Wait', he says. 'Let me take you home.'

'Where do you live?'

'Just two blocks down.'

'Okay.' We don't turn the lights on when we get there. He's sobered up enough to take the reins, his hands pressing on my shoulders, steering me. He stops in the middle of the pitch-black hallway, embracing me from behind, pressing kisses on the side of my neck.

'That's not what I asked you to do.' There's a challenge in my tone, and it works just right. I need another fight to pick. He pushes me into the bedroom, against the wall, and throws me onto the bed. I'm struggling in form, but really I'm just drowning.

'Shit', he says, stilling for a moment. 'I don't have a-'

'No', I interject, and my hands are already smoothing him over, negotiating. 'Please. I need it'. That's all the coaxing he needs.

17

I wake up with a sandpaper tongue, straining to open my eyes. The blinds are drawn, but sunlight is streaming in. A man's arm snakes across my chest, heavy with sleep and sweat. His face is turned away, and there is a tattoo on his neck. I close my eyes and try to grasp at the night, but nothing comes back to me, a nothing so complete it makes me shiver. There is a shape slithering underneath, but I can't possess it.

My coat is bundled on the floor. I check the pockets: keys, phone, with its battery is only quarter-dead. A notification flashes at me - fuck, I've got fifteen minutes. I dress myself frantically and run out of the door. On the steps in front of his building, I breathe a sigh of relief. At least the place is central. I glance at my reflection on the windows of a department store. My dress is too short for a job interview, but the real problem is the tangled hair, the dark circles beneath my eyes, the half-moon scratch mark on my cheekbone. I'll have to win them over with my personality, I mouth at the dirty glass, and the mere shape of the words makes me wince.

An expressionless teenager shows me through to the cramped backroom of the café. The manager remains seated at her desk and stares at me with unveiled disdain. Her fake pearl necklace is so shiny it makes me imagine her kneeling by her bed at night, polishing the individual spheres like a rosary. Her own surface looks uncracked, too.

'Lydia?'

'Yes.'

'Take a seat.'

'Thank you for having me.'

'My pleasure.' Her eyes glaze over her print-out of my pitiful CV. 'So tell me, how much café experience do you have?'

'I used to work at a service station. It involved making and serving coffee.'

'Not the kind of coffee we serve, I presume.'

'I'm a quick learner.'

'You're going to have to work under pressure.'

'I'm used to that. I like having something to fight against. Not that I'm an aggressive person. It's just a figure of speech.'

'Ms. Ellis?'

A nurse is poking her head out of the door.

I glance around rapidly. PLANNING TO SCORE? a bright green poster asks on the wall to my right. A basket of condoms is laid out on a table like a bowl of candy for trick-and-treaters.

'Ms. Ellis?' the nurse repeats, looking at me like she knows me.

'I'm here', I say, getting up.

In the treatment room, she pulls up my file on the computer.

'You booked in for an STD test, but it's only been two months since your previous one. We don't usually recommend doing them that often. I assume there has been a change in your circumstances?'

I nod.

'Have you been assaulted? We have a process for - if you need any support.'

'I don't want to talk about it.'

'Are you sure?'

'Yes.' I know I've been irresponsible. Not me, but something in me, and really it's all me. I'm not sure it matters that much. Only it matters more than anything else in the world.

'Let's get some bloods as well', the nurse says.

I go home, and the fridge door is smeared all over with strawberry jam. I glide my finger over the surface, sweetened dermis, and lick it. It's thick and strangely bitter.

The tape breaks, and the frequency of static has changed. I'm at a party, leaning against a wall with a glass of wine in my hand. I know I have been here for a while, holding a conversation with a guy with whom I once went on a boring first date.

I can't remember his name. He is looking at me expectantly, but I'm not sure what we've been talking about, if anything, so I say the first thing that comes to mind.

'Recently I've been so horny for domesticity.'

'Really?'

'I've had it in the past, briefly, and it's always slipped through my fingers. Nothing ever feels like it's meant to last, and that's the beauty of it. That's what I should hold on to. But I want to be devoted to someone. Maybe it's just because it's late summer, but I want to settle down a little.'

'That's unexpected.'

'Why are you surprised?

'Well, you have a habit of making people feel like they're just a very small part of your life. Like you have something colourful and exciting going on all the time, and they're just a footnote at best.'

While he speaks, his mouth twists into a horrible long-suffering smile I've seen before. He is beautiful and I want him to run away from me. Still, I can't make myself push hard enough.

'I'm just being honest. It's not supposed to be an excuse, or a jab. If anything, it's a challenge. I'm saying look, I'm not going to just sit at home and wait for you. I've got too much to give. But if I'm talking to you about my love life at all, that means I already give a fuck about you. So if you can take me, you can have me.'

'It's a lot to take in.'

'Trust me, I know. I need to find someone who can defeat me.'

'Do you ever feel like you were born in the wrong era?'

'Huh?'

'Maybe men used to be harder.' I feel the gears of the conversation turning, shifting into a two-way exchange of fantasies, and it makes me a little hot in the face.

'I have no interest in life between a fist and a stove. It's got to be a fair fight.'

'But you admit you're looking for a fighter.'

'Sort of. I guess.' All I want is the pure thrill of a hostile world, begging it to swallow me, bones and all.

There is a birthday cake on a glass table, colourful cards scattered around it. I recognise my old classmates' faces. All of them are smiling.

Time won't heal a girl who loves to hide.

'Are things OK between us, now?' Alice asks. 'Am I allowed to speak to you?'

It takes me a while to realise she's talking to me.

'Of course', I say, bewildered by the question. 'You can speak to me anytime.'

The way she looks down at her shoes, her brow furrowed in frustration or embarrassment, makes my heart sink. I've always cared about Alice. I used to crush on her in school, cling to her like glue, until things got weird. Now, we're almost like siblings. She's from a good family, one I could never really belong to. She's studying philosophy in the capital, writing long essays on the pain of being. When I'm alone and I think about her, I feel so proud it makes me tear up.

'You didn't respond to my texts for weeks, and I asked around, but nobody knew what you were up to. I wanted to come banging on your door, but the spring term was so busy I couldn't make the trip. I kept trying to call, to make sure you're OK. When you finally responded, you sounded really angry. You told me to never call again.'

'I'm so sorry.'

She looks me straight in the eye. 'Do you not remember?'

I shake my head, and she sighs.

'You're getting it wrong', I say. 'I wasn't fucked up - not like that. My head's just been a mess.'

Changed my mind again, bleaching carpets until all that remains are the stains. 'It was blood, wasn't it?' I ask my mother, and she just shakes her head. I have the scars to prove her wrong. It just takes me a while to find them.

Now my cut glass fingers beckon disease, little murders.

'You're splitting again?' Alice whispers, glancing around as though she's afraid of our conversation being overheard. The buzz of other voices continues reassuringly. I'm not scared to tell the truth, anyway. I could tell every single person in the room that I'm insane and not even flinch.

'Guess so. Yes.'

'I'm sorry to hear that.'

I wave my hand dismissively. 'Don't say that. You don't have to worry about me. I'm okay.'

'But are you staying safe?'

Maybe it's fucked up, how my mind only knows to protect itself by terrorising my body. But whatever happens, I am in charge, only me, an indivisible multitude, and I refuse to be afraid of myself.

Mercifully, my phone rings - a callback from the café. They want me to start on Monday. I suppose they have taken pity on me, for being a 22-year-old NEET with a bruised face and tatty clothes. They don't even know half of it. Still, it calls for a celebration.

A text from my dad flashes on my overheated phone: Would be great if you could pay me back ASAP so I don't have to sue you in small claims court.

Even when I am fully in myself, present tense, I am always observing the world through a screen, transparent but slightly clouded. I forget it is there, but sooner or later, I catch a reflection. Sometimes I've desperately wanted to punch through it, to know how it really feels to be in this skin, how it feels to feel, but I understand it is a blessing. Pain experienced through the veil is subdivided by it - I only get the aftershock. Such as this. A little shiver. Far from the kind of death rattle my sister might have experienced.

My cheek rests against something very cold. My teeth are chattering, and with each little movement my face bumps against the hard surface, causing some pain. My panties are bunched at my ankles, and my pulse is very fast, faster than the beat flowing through the walls.

There's a knock on the bathroom door.

'Is someone in there?'

I don't want to keep them waiting, but I don't know where my voice is. It's so loud outside. I would have to shout to be heard.

Another bang. Bang. Bang.

'Fuck off!' I mouth.

The noise from outside goes into my head and scrambles it so the boundaries between past and present leak like a ghost ship. I am being kissed against the door, my neck straining in a weird angle - now the blood beats against my skin like it's out for revenge for what - I am on my knees, closed, open, my head lolls back and I'm not there. What did they look like? What were they looking for? I know their fingers were rough. I shoved them out, locked the door behind them. Good riddance. Their face, the way we fucked, if we fucked, all of it gone. Shouldn't get my panties in a bunch, ha, but suddenly it's driving me crazy, the face-lessness of my memory. Who the fuck was it? Why this again?

24

The door rattles, the people outside are kicking it now. If I walk out there will I recognise the person who claimed me? Will they claim me again? Will I pick some other person without a name and let them do anything they want to me and wilfully forget all about it?

I get up on shaky legs and walk to the window. The roof of the garage is just underneath it. Softly softly, I open the window and slip through it. They can kick the door down and see I was never really there.

Another conversation. I can't do this anymore. 'Please just let me listen', I say.

My friends look at me, bemused. 'That sounds wrong, coming from you.'

I walk into a corner of the living room, laughing and choking back tears. Ever so perceptive, Alice asks: 'Is everything okay?'

'Yeah. I'm dealing with it', I say.

'With what? Has something happened?' Lucy asks, shrill and annoying.

'Nothing.' I shake my head wetly, like a dog that has just crawled its way back ashore.

'You seemed a lot better when you came in', she continues.

'OK, thanks. I'll send my regards to whoever was in charge of this meat vessel.'

'I saw a TikTok the other day about systems therapy-'

'I'm not on fucking TikTok.' I rub my face with my left hand. 'I'm sorry. I'm just tired.' Desperate to busy my hands with something, I latch onto the phone in my pocket. Seven missed calls from the café. I must have missed my first shift, or set the place on fire. I'm not sure which would feel worse.

Alice takes me down to the river. She lets me drink a couple glasses of vodka before confiscating my card.

'Can you tell me', I say, and the earnestness of my tone makes me cringe despite the alcohol, 'What is the difference between dissociation and transcendence?'

'That's a big question', she says.

'You know I barely got a middle school leaving certificate. Anything you say will be above my level', I say, and although it sounds sycophantic, I mean it. Alice's face is blushed, but I don't think she feels that intimidated by my question. It must be the matte Merlot staining her lips. I hold my breath while she gathers her thoughts.

'Transcendence is divine, going beyond your usual self - leaving it behind for something better. A state of enlightenment. Dissociation is its twisted mirror, preventing you from knowing and developing yourself.'

'Okay', I say. 'But it feels like enlightenment, sometimes. It feels like I'm touching something that I'm not allowed to - something vast and forbidden. It's just beneath the surface. I get so close to understanding.'

It is more a womb than a void, whatever it is, birthing me over and over again. The residue of lost time sticks to me like bits of placenta. Can they smell it on me? I watch myself go, over and over again, saintly touring clinics and pharmacies. Mea culpa, corpus meum, holier with every resurrection, and less whole. I know I am closest to God when I lose myself in vacuums.

'It sounds intense', Alice says.

'I'm so glad you don't know what it's like.'

There must be something wrong with my face, because Alice looks away and pulls me closer, suddenly embracing me so warm and tight it knocks the breath out of me. My eyes are stinging with tears. I am here now only here only now maybe I can stay for a little longer.

WHIPLASH

I see the change in me
through your eyes
in this disinfected corridor
my body is the same

paper skin steel blades hide soft entrails
the last time I was desperate and insane

obscure interlude
something wrong

I want to drop the subterfuge
grab your little ponytail drag you along

'I am glad to see you.'   'I wish I could say the same.'

but my memory lies buried in these walls

'I've been in bed all week. They're changing my meds and it's made me
into a sleepwalker.'
'You seem perfectly awake now.'
'Lucky you, catching me at my most alert.'

Your bright eyes measure the distance between us,
what I had to forget: the bitter red roots of a house,
a burning acrid alphabet.

'You'll get out, too.'
'I am scared of leaving.'
'Everyone is.'

Because I am not here I can be there for you.
Will I?
Am I a coward, failing to be embraced
by the warm glow of promises?

Rainy alcoves, streetcorners
by shining marble floodgates.
Ruined mattress, silent murders,
bloodsoaked slates consecrates
at the faculty of history.

In nightclub smokerooms,
validate my hysterie.
Wet eyes red eyes even eyes
used to hold my reflection
now I must look away.

These memories an oil spill
contaminating all I have purified.
Underneath I only feel their shape
with jagged edges unsterilised.

'I'll be there for you',
but there is no guarantee
such a crude binary

when I was desperate only you could touch me
now you're a sliver of shadow
a dead decree

Uniform of Affection

So fulfilling, to hold a fuchsia cloud of feathers
white lace apron tight against my waist
dusting every corner of the dream house
I say please. Miss. Can this be homemaking

Shock collar on my thigh sings
Love is tough. Here, you can earn it.
Miss, she looks at me and smiles
All the best angels are monstrous.

Somewhere a family sits down for a meal
No flowers at the table, just soft steam rising
from chipped stoneware, a stained jug of water
being lifted, an image I fetishise

Sometimes, I'm invited to the tableau.
All words are foreign on my tongue
except - thank you. Thank you.
Surely you see I don't belong here.

I will swallow my fill. I will feel hollow again,
bake a fool's gold crust for the mincemeat
of my heart, crumbs for a grotesque
Gretel chasing the glow of a hearth

REAPER

Eros a forcefield shedding repelling consuming skin-
shadows desperate to incarnate, open nerve endings
the world pretends to be a closed circuit
red thread moving from my wrist
to my throat, pulling tight
vital dissonance

I dreamt in negatives
explosive equilibrium
destroyed by other
awaken prismatic
supercharging lovelust
dispersed in all things
return to me so bright
yet never blinding
shatter two-way glass
walk all over it with bare feet
feel it - a caress.

Even the October light grows hesitant
to witness decay, softening
the colour of rotten leaves
underfoot. Morning darkness
gilded death in clouded mirrors
nothing as unspeakable as desire
to belong

SLEEP SONG

I wanted my fury to flourish into a frozen flower, self-possessed, blue head held high. I could not find the seed. It must have melted in the hot rush of my blood, over and over and over again,

until that golden afternoon I crushed a peach in my fist. My sticky fingers shook, but for once, my words were untrembling.

'You treated me badly'.

'I know. I'm sorry',

enough hot air to suffocate this pitiful fire I tended. My heavy feet sunk through the sun-speckled sidewalk

down down down

in the black river waters I slept for awhile.

Nobody has hurt me like that before you. I have many things to confess. Maybe I was trying to finish what you started. I remember how it was, your voice taut with hatred on the crackling phone line. I would rather take endless silence.

I want to come up with a new dance, something funny, an excuse for your arms around my waist. Please let's never forgive each other again. Let's not be friends. I want you as you are now to see me as I am now; I want to see your cold eyes reflect me undistorted.

The dream had been steering me and I saw it for its red emptiness, how it had bled me dry - stillborn something in the cradle of skin, the shock of my old life in my hands leaving traces on you throbbing in the synthetic fibers of your coat. Could you feel it through the fabric, my stain? How my dream screamed at you, begged to be kept on life support. You cut the cord and walked away.

I could spend the rest of eternity constructing the machine, and it would never turn me on. Marked on the blueprint of myopia, I'd find the x x xxxxx a rainy Monday morning, numb fingers, an ache

I know I am not dead yet because I see the grave, right there for me to climb into, and I look down at it and I look at my hands and I see the gutted dream gleaming

hole dug into soil rippling with worms. I think I could only love you before I was really born. I thought that was the loudest my blood could ever be and I was wrong. It is drawing something new, never afraid of the dark,

only curious - funny, how blindly I could sink into the quicksand of night, and look back over the bone of my bitten shoulder, straight into the neon eyes of warning signs, advertisements of exuberant regret, hands on my hips, guiding me, limbs diverging, a tree that cut itself down the middle

on the contrary - I thought I must live in the shadow of something tall and capable of cruelty, to be safekept by choice. In the chaos of this world, to close my eyes within the misè-en-scene of chromosomes, a familiar madness, kill switch mechanisms remystified.

EUTROPHICATION WALTZ

dance broken over poisoned waters
shoredrifted shinbones, lungs
blooming blue-green algae in the shallows
metal rippled tongues salt crystallised skins
dance until your blood stops breathing

Wheeling out the sun-yellow sharpbox,
comrade-in-arms of the needle container,
you ask if I'm scared. I say No
The shivering is just because I'm cold.
(I mean it.) You ask if I can take twenty-five.

Your gaze, molten candlewax
dripping down my breasts.
I say y e s (please, please). (small sigh).

You thread the first stanza of needles
into the top of my right thigh,
a refrain for the left.

Breathing in and out,
twenty-two pierced in the soft flesh
of my legs now. Fierce little fencers.
And the terminal trio?
You browse the possibilities
of my pain-abiding body (flashes of lustful delirium:
would you sew my lips shut? My eyelids open?)

You adorn my nipples with a pretty, pink-gauged pair,
too gently? My gut tells me you're holding fury for the finale.
Yet I can't help gasping as you insert the last thorn
in the softest part of me, just above the navel.

'Don't move. You don't want to stab yourself in the stomach, do you?'
I shake my head, my whole body shakes the more I will it
into stillness flesh quivers, stubborn; weak
yet skin stretches over metal thin, intact, resisting
until we perform the strange slow dance of pulling them out,
blood blooming in their wake. All for you to smear
over the surface of me. Over your canvas:
a smudge on the lips of the painted woman, the murderess,
my body blending with its image, suddenly weightless,
euphoric to bleed for you. For you to take what's inside,
make it beautiful. Write secret letters under my dress.

I HAVE NO NEED FOR A MAN INSIDE THE LEATHER JACKET

the scent suffices, the warmth
of skin on skin, creaking
folds of flesh
a long-dead thing
comforting

this animal that never had a name
never slept beside its mother
holding me so tight
i smell like love

My Love Is of My Body (an Unholy Seep)

Today, the snowdrops in the yard cower under a freezing sun, petrified. I wonder if that is a predictor of my mistress' mood.

After I'm through the threshold, I take off my heels to make sure their sharp click on the floor won't wake her up, tiptoe to the kitchen to put the kettle on. She is already sitting on the windowsill and smoking morosely.

'Good morning, Mistress', I say. 'I'm surprised to see you awake so early.'
'I didn't get much sleep', she says. 'There's a lot on my mind.'
'I hope I am not disturbing you.'
She looks at me with a glimmer in her eye.
'I see you're Marlene today. Oh, I really like that dress.'
'Thank you, Mistress.'

I always thought she would view this dress, black satin with a white lace collar and an apron, as a signifier obvious enough to be drab and meaningless. Something you might buy in a novelty shop or glimpse in dime-a-dozen pornography, worn only to be discarded.

The Slutty Maid. At the same time, I am delighted she likes it; inhibiting a stock character has its comforts. I could not exist like this around anyone else.

'There is something I want you to do for me, little maid. I have a new project on my mind', she says.
'Of course, Mistress.'
I look at her in expectation, but no details are forthcoming.
'I will tell you when you serve me my afternoon tea.'
I lower my gaze. 'I look forward to it, Mistress.'

I am on my knees in the living room, watching the freshly polished floorboards glitter, when Mistress walks up to me from behind and grabs my ponytail. While yanking it, she bends down and says, very close to my ear: 'Excellent work, my sweet maid. I think you deserve a treat.'

I feel something warm pressing against my throat and quickly recognise it as the leather of my collar. She closes the clasp at the back of my neck and plants a little kiss on the top of my spine, exposed by the flimsy dress. I close my eyes and breathe softly. A sound like windchimes rings in my ears: Mistress is handling the silver chain, an object of comfort. She attaches it to the front of my collar and embraces me for a moment, one hand holding the leash, the other spreading its fingers over my clothed chest. I wonder if she can feel my pulse through the white lace chemise. The longer she touches me the more arrhythmical my heart becomes, losing all sense of time. All of me goes stupid. Mistress straightens her back and the firm press of her fingers is gone, but the leash still binds us together.

'Come on now, kitten. You'll get some dessert.'

She yanks the chain, dragging me towards the kitchen on all fours. I love the sound of my nylon-covered knees bumping into the hard floorboards, my elbows clumsily falling on the surface beneath. Mistress' legs are so strong and beautiful. She could lead me anywhere, tirelessly; but I want nothing more than to make things easier for her.

She has laid out a little bowl on the centre of the kitchen floor and filled it with white liquid I can only assume to be milk. I position myself in front of the bowl on all fours, stretching my spine, as coy and feline as I can be.

'Show me your cute little tongue.'

I open my mouth and extend my langue-de-chat for inspection. Smiling, my mistress kneels beside me. She takes the pink slip of it between her index and middle finger, squeezing tight. I look at her with wide eyes. She brings her face closer and entwines my tongue with her own, tasting of ash and oranges. It is a violent kiss – her teeth scrape my lips, and as a final note, she bites down hard enough to make me bleed. While I suck on my wounded tongue, Mistress gets up and gives my chain an encouraging tug. 'Now put it to work. Drink up, kitten.'

When my tongue breaks the smooth surface of the liquid, a crimson swirl appears in it. I lap up the pink milk, savouring the sweetness and the iron tang of it.

'You are making a mess', Mistress says. It's true, I can't help it – milk drips down my chin, splashes on the floor. I am not sure if I should stop to apologise or continue performing my task. Persistence seems the greater virtue. I keep licking until the empty bowl floats in a creamy white puddle.

'How can you present yourself as a maid when you're such a nasty messy girl? Talk about false advertising. Clean it up, bitch', Mistress says.

I get to work slurping and lapping the milk from the floor. The surface of it feels rough against my wounded tongue. My entire being is focused on completing this task: nothing exists in the world except for the pool of blood-milk and my mistress watching over me. 'You're not going to cry about the spilled milk? What a shame. I should've cut your tongue with a knife instead.'

Afterwards, I serve both of us tea in dainty little porcelain cups. Mistress makes me swirl the hot liquid in my mouth, making sure I thoroughly scald the wound. My eyes water, and she looks at me so fondly I am overwhelmed.

'I want to write a poem with you, Marlene', she says.
'But, Mistress, I'm no good at writing.'
'Sshh. We all have our virtues.'
'How could I help you with this?'
'Your blood will be my ink.'
'That must be the nicest thing anyone has ever said to me.'

'Don't make me blush, Marlene. If you want to show your appreciation, get on your knees under the table.'

Overcome by a rush of affection, I crawl into the tight space under the dining table and slide her black satin panties down. Already wet with both blood and arousal, Mistress grips my head between her hands, fucking herself on my mouth so relentlessly that I come close to choking on her cunt. I keep licking until my tongue is awfully sore and my face is drenched in her cum and her womb lining. The taste and smell of her are driving me crazy, and it takes every last drop of my self-restraint to keep my hands on my lap. Patience is not one of my virtues, but I will practice it for her.

Truth be told, I have abandoned all faith in natural virtue. Before I found Mistress, I followed the will of a man who believed in the sanctity of female suffering. In my desire to be Good, I wore the straitjacket of victimhood, resigning myself to violation after violation. One day, I heard he had hurt a dear friend of mine. I voiced my distress: her anguish was my anguish. Vampirically stealing our pain for himself, he said that my accusations gravely offended him; he demanded I kneel down before him and apologise. Incandescent with rage, I shot him through the heart. While his carcass was still ebbing with warmth, I dug my fingers deep into the hole in his chest, twisting them into the firm tissue of his heart. It yielded under my touch, weak as expected. I smeared the remains of his pathetic heart on my face and swore I would never again submit to anyone who expected it on the basis of my sex.

Mistress understands the depth of my rage. My pistol lies in the bottom of my suitcase, silent.

I have nearly finished cleaning the tub when she enters the bathroom, a beaming smile on her face.

'Inspiration has struck me', she says and extends her hand. 'Come'.

I peel off the disposable gloves and let her walk me downstairs. In the middle of the conservatory, Mistress has set out a single chair and a small table. A transparent container of needles sits atop the table, drawing my eye.

'I will go get some supplies', Mistress says. 'I want you undressed and waiting for me in that chair by the time I'm back.'

I untie my apron and take off my dress, shivering in anticipation. By the time she enters the room with a gleaming white sharpbox, I am sitting prim and nude in the chair, immobile as though I were already restrained.

'Straighten your back', Mistress says while she binds my wrists to the chair with a leather belt. 'Show respect for me with your posture.'

'Yes, Mistress.'
'Now, are you sure you want to give me this gift?'
'Yes, Mistress, I want this so much.'
'Good. I like it when my servants are eager to please. Let's get started, then.'

When my vision goes dim, it's not blood loss but an exaltation. I have lost count of the needles that have been stuck in my flesh: there may be forty or fifty of them, the Devil is in the details, and I welcome Her.

'You would make a pretty picture like that', Mistress says. I gaze at a long needle inserted horizontally above my navel. 'Let me get my camera. Don't fool around and stab yourself while I'm gone'. I remain transfixed by the needle as Mistress goes and comes, immortalising my trance. I can barely remember what my face looks like. It does not matter now that my flesh has become a vessel for something I cannot quite pronounce.

Slowly, Mistress starts pulling out the needles in my thighs, blood blooming in their wake. The smell of it makes me feel close to the earth, full of life. A thin wood-handled brush dangles in Mistress' fingers. She dips its bristles into the expanding pool of red on my left thigh, transferring my life-force between the containers of my body and her canvas. It is angled away from me so I cannot see the words she is writing – it might just as well be a love poem about me, or about another girl in her past; an ode to the snowdrops in the yard; an oath of revenge –the lack of knowledge doesn't bother me in the slightest. She could use me up, consume me like this, for whatever purpose she deems fit. I trust her with my life, my death, everything.

My love is of my body, and the blood rising to my surface must be permeated by it. Most of the needles have been taken out now, the canvas of my skin filled with colour. Mistress' hands are stained with the deep red of me, too, and I cannot stop wondering if the love in my DNA is seeping through her epidermis. Sometimes it feels like a disease, wanting to give myself to her so completely.

What if I am transmitting it – what if those bloody palms hold biohazard psalms? And what about all the fury coursing in my veins? If I make my Mistress more wrathful, I will gladly suffer the consequences, but I don't want her to suffer from love.

'What are you thinking of?' I ask.

Is my love contagious? Is it dangerous?

'Oh, silly things, Mistress. I feel so blissful.'

'You've been so good to me, Marlene. So beautiful. You deserve a world of pain after this.'

EMPTY POOL

Scraping paint to uncover stretch marks underneath
How did this house grow so vast?
Looming over every other dream
somewhere I'm swimming laps
and it's all dripping thick carmine
Dissolving in the pool of nail polish
she spilt in the bathroom corner
drawing acid baths at the foot of the washer
twenty-year hangover. Death in midsummer
Skimming a layer of putrefaction
off the top of the milk in her kitchen
It is in my muscle memory to drink it
like swallowing a creamy sunbeam.
Now the edges of every room are fraying
softer, softer. Sticking to my throat
a burning smell. A fire of days.

Heatwave Diary

These are the days I feel the most alive
Walking down burning streets with sticky skin
and a parched mouth, heart throbbing a throwaway disco track
swallowing lingering spit and smoke and sunscreen

The rind of the world swells overripe
Exhaling sewage and floral putrefaction
My body hums with the ease of expiration
Inhaling the heatwave creep of death

The presence, the danger of that precipice
throwing my aliveness to stark relief.
Thighs rubbing together under my skirt
making me itch with a hollow urge
to pare them down with a knife,
a venomous purge. I despise thermal expansion,
feeling fleshy boundaries liquefy.
The sun is a glinting blade, and I look away.

I don't reject all the world,
just parts of it,
but they still seep through to me.

Should I just accept it, everything?

I am so porous, just like the dried-up sunbloom on my palm,
just like the translucent caterpillar failing to receive any nourishment
from it.

These things are real and warm and dry in my hand.
I like holding onto them in the face of ungraspable things,
closing my fist.

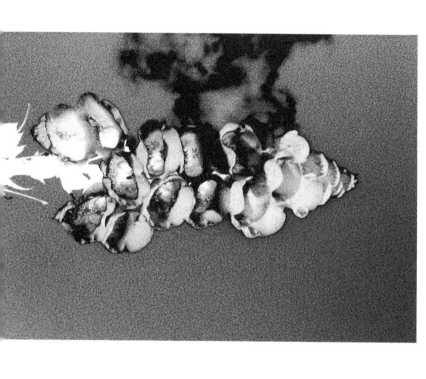

HOTHOUSE CAMELLIA (FOR A GIRL OF CELLULOID)

The trembling funambulist walks past her Mother floating in the aquarium, a tangle of white ankles and Calla lilies. Silver pennies fall through the mass of water, flipped high into the air by her audience. Every time one slides into the coin slot of Mother's mouth, her pretty face contorts. The funambulist imagines a knife gliding through her wet and slippery gut, spilling a fortune of rusted scales.

The funambulist's brother rides a red-hot comet, scaling the walls of death thrice a day. The afterglow of his blaze comes from light years away. Before her own show, she watches the glittering dust trail in the night sky, a faceless memory.

In the darkness she walks in, the silent shutter of her lids is a flash of gold. The rope burns warnings into her soft soles as silhouettes hold their breath. With her eyes closed, the funambulist sees a single star, paper birch, pale against the sky. She watches it twinkling at the very end of her rope, a sweet reunion, perpendicular bloodlines bending to bring her home.

WHAT I MUST DO

Today I woke and stepped into the solar X-ray.
There is nothing broken inside you it said
You are luminous
The warmth was too much to take.

Signs of spring: flowers, bruises.
Distracted fingers weaving threads
of mottled lilac memories

Last night a man from the foreign office hurt me
just because I asked him
(if I ever let a man from the home office do that to me
I should die of shame)
caned me bloodlessly,
disinterested in my suffering.
Beautiful.

I thought I must be done with the vampires
because I would let them suck me dry,
use me right up. Extinguish me.
I would say thank you, or most likely
negate my self into a thing shivering silent
unfeeling. I would lose my words.
Yet I must not. My friends tell me –
sometimes I tell me –

I must give to those who take in communion
my love, a spring. Drink from it,
spit in my mouth. Receive with grace

I shall leave this body. Not in little death but a little rebirth

blooming bells toll for me
grey sky pushes down
brilliant chaos petals
resisting
breathing in a violent blossom
fill me with spring

pale of long days outside
glistening. chained to skin
thorns break me
explode in colour

without the signs i am seeing
in darkrooms gazes give birth to true memories
behind glass walls. labyrinth of translucency
never ever find the soul
afterall the function of ink is to stain things
a mess a mass of true blue darkness
a static of incoherence
in words i am not alive and neither are you

Any city is a city of heartbreak if you stay long enough
恋の予感は失恋の予感 / but I have changed.
I want to walk through the ruins with a smile
see grey cathedrals of capital glorified by the light of loss
the marbled walls of this centrifugal heart
morph into pulsating aortae, bleak pavements
flush with warm blood, whispering
It's not over. It's not over.
Watch me let in the cold light
Let it wash over you, through you
You will never be held, here
Isn't that what you want
誰にも見せない冷えた焼跡の寂静

Inner Light

The world has shifted beyond recognition again.
I've been sketching an alla prima rendering of a memory: my child-self
bending down on a piano stool, being whipped with a leather belt. An
explosion of purple. In the blink of an eye, the colours have drained.
Not just the bruises, everything, on and off canvas. My hands have
turned into ash.

I felt something like this in the park after the parade, only in full techni-
colour. My body grew midsummer roses, my own thorns cut into me. I
cut a key-shaped hole in my chest and watched the movements of that
exotic fish in a fleshy aquarium, my heart. That had been the last of the
tabs I'd bought off Mel; there is nothing left in the house, now.

Have I been inhaling the paintings? Frantically, I look for clues in the
tubes of gouache strewn about my desk. Gum Arabic. Polyethylene Gly-
col. Titanium White. Benzisothiazolinone. Non Toxic.

Titanium white is only used in trace amounts to produce certain colours,
including Cadmium Lemon Yellow, Naples Yellow, and Cobalt Blue Hue.
I recognize these tubes by reading the words written on the tubes in
small print.
I rub my eyes sore and blink until they water, but the grayscale world will
not revividify.

All my life, I have prided myself on being someone who processes shit
by throwing myself deeper into it. I'll absorb the meanest suckerpunch
with glee. My knees meet the floor with a hollow little sound. Is this
psychosis?

There are few things as terrifying as going crazy. I've always feared I might be doomed for late-onset schizophrenia, ever since my blood mother started hearing voices and threatening us with rifles. She took a penitentiary detour to the medicated lifestyle, but she's fine now. We are all fine now.

I've worked on this sequence all summer, no, all my life – it is my life – and there is no way an uninvited bout of insanity will stop me. Yet my flesh is weaker, or at least more incompetent, than my spirit, and it takes less than half an hour to discover I'm no Sargy Mann. Theoretically, I know which colour to use where, as all the information I need is written on the little tubes. I can observe the gradation of hues, the mother's face (not my mother) in the shadows, the texture of paint in various stages of drying. Still, painting in a grey world is like fucking the girl of all your dreams, but your flesh is suddenly replaced with a cheap plastic strap-on in a poorly fitting harness. Not that I know how that feels. All I understand is that painting grey bruises, grey piano keys, grey foxgloves, is misery.

'There is nothing concerning in your OCT scan', the ophthalmologist says. 'Your maculae and your optic nerves are perfectly healthy.'

'Oh', I say.

'Do you feel there has been a change in your vision?'

I shake my head. 'Nothing major. It's just a little blurry.'

'Your eyesight is above average. There's just one thing – your meibomian glands, on the rim of the eye, are slightly blocked. Your eyes are not producing enough moisture.'

'I should probably cry more.'

'That would actually make it worse. What you should do is cover your eyes with a hot towel. Do it for ten minutes before bed, every night.'

My walk home takes me past the canal (liquid mercury), and the flower market (overflowing with petrified moon blooms). I buy tinted sunglasses to switch into a different palette of monochrome, but it barely augments my sense of reality.

At home, I microwave the expensive compress towel the ophthalmologist sold me, lie on top of the bed and hide in total darkness. I listen through Le Poème de l'Extase once, then reheat the compress and do it all over again. Time passes strangely, multiclimatically. Divinely fouled up. All fire and air. Recalling that Scriabin was a synesthete, I think very hard of sound waves traversing the visible spectrum, trying to colour in the viscous topology of chords. From a dark cavern I shall ascend to witness an ultramarine bliss. After the orgy winds down, I peel off the compress. My stomach barely sinks at all: I always knew it wouldn't work.

I'm on a deadline. I'm always on a fucking deadline, but this time it's really important. It's my first post-graduation group show, and only one piece of my little trifecta is finished. I've let my rage seep into the canvas undiluted, and it's been going surprisingly well. Maybe this is a sign from the Universe, big black neon letters saying

DROP THE BRUSH AND GO DIE IN A DITCH SOMEWHERE, NOBODY CARES ABOUT YOUR CHILDHOOD TRAUMA. Obeying direct commands has never been my strong suit, though. If Gxd really wanted to mess with me, () should at least attempt some reverse psychology. I'm all for mind fucks, but this is quite literally dull.

In a weak attempt to break through my self-pity, I make a cup of coffee. I balance a silver filter on a white mug and take my time gazing at the blooming grounds, the sheen of oil on the surface, comfortingly unchanged. The medicine is not sweet enough to placate my despair, though. I can't paint, the clock is ticking too loudly, and the walls are closing in on me. This white noise buzz of anxiety can only be killed with something louder.

I've become well-adjusted in that wired way formerly hopeless people tend to be. Short-circuiting seems inevitable.

Still, a changed world must result in a changed self, which is how I justify the razorblade on my inner arm, hesitating like a lapsing vegan. A beast will always remember its nature. I close my eyes for the first graze, and open them for a miracle. I've never flinched at the sight of my own blood before. Within the virginal stain licking its way down the slate of my elbow, the shock of crimson reveals other colours, breathtaking. I can hardly believe all this has come from my veins. Bewitched, I rush into my workroom and grab a fine sable brush. I must have always underestimated my inner beauty, so brilliant against the coarse linen of the canvas. I get no further than outlining a human figure kneeling on an ornate clock face before my head starts feeling dangerously light. Resigned, I take out a first-aid kit and make a tight cradle of gauze for my arm.

After devouring a chocolate bar, I go cruising for materials. It's getting dark out, and I'm in a pre-code noir film. Anything could happen.

As I walk through the warehouse district, a sharp odour draws my attention. I circle around the imposing buildings until its source reveals itself to me: a grey building with a corrugated iron front. Ascending the steps, I notice that the chain lock on the door has already been cut by someone on a misadventure of their own. I stick my head in and let my eyes get used to the heady metallic darkness. A former abattoir. If it wasn't for the smell, I might think the floor is stained with sticky ink. I take out my phone and switch on the torch. The stains swallow the light I shine on them, refracting no beauty at all. Evidently, not just any old blood will do.

I keep walking, gazing up at a celluloid sky, until I find myself standing across the street from Vic's bar, watching unwashed undergrads spill into the street. Unfortunately, it's the best bet for finding someone romantic or unhinged enough to take this kind of thing in stride.

On cue, a bell-bright voice chimes from behind me: 'Hey, Rebecca! I haven't seen you in ages!'

'Hi', I say, turning around to flash a smile at a round-faced blonde. I vaguely remember tutoring a class she attended last winter, but her name evades me. 'Good to see you – Millie?'

'Lucy', she says with an unwavering smile. 'How have you been?'

'Oh, extremely busy.'

'What happened to your arm?'

'Nothing serious. Got clawed by an alley cat.'

Lucy's face twists into a little grimace of sympathy. 'I hope you've got your tetanus shots. Anyway, I heard you're doing a show at Faith next month. That's so cool.'

'You should come to the opening night.' I take stock of the way she holds her breath while looking at me. Her infatuation is embarrassingly obvious. 'To be honest, I'd love to spend some time with you before then.'

'I'd love that too', Lucy exhales.

'Want to come to my studio?'

'Right now?'

'Yeah.'

'My friends are inside, but-' She glances towards the bar and sighs. 'Fuck it.'

It's a strange mix of fortunes today. I start walking, looking behind my shoulder to check she's following. Her eyes flicker coyly between me and her white mary janes. I pick up the pace and she trudges along, awkward in her platform shoes.

'I feel like a kidnapper.'

'Why?'

'You're too young for me.'

'I'm just two years younger than you.'

'But you seem so innocent. Is it an act?'

'I don't know. I've done some stuff.'

'Like what?'

'I'm not a virgin.'

'I'm not interested in having sex with you.'

'Oh.' There is a note of relief in Lucy's voice, or maybe I'm just imagining it, having already typecast her in the role of a long-suffering waif. We pass a park with the street lamps all unlit, thickets rustling with wind and sweaty limbs. I extend my hand, and Lucy takes it.

'Actually, I want to know if you will do me a favour.' I stare down at her, purposefully intense. I wonder if her eyes are blue or green – the colour is almost pale enough to blend in with her sclera.

'What kind of a favour?'

'I'm not going to think any less of you if you say no. I know this is strange.'

'You've warned me. What is it?'

'Could I please paint with your blood?'

'Oh', Lucy says, and a dopey smile spreads across her face. 'Yes'.

'I'm not going to hurt you', I say. 'I just need a little bit. I'm trying something new.'

'You can hurt me if you like. You could even kill me and I wouldn't mind.'

A protective urge washes over me, taking the shape of anger. 'That's really fucked up. Don't say that.'

'Okay.'

'There are lots of people who would run wild with it, and it's ugly as hell. Have some self-respect.'

'Okay.'

'I'm not trying to preach from a moral high ground here. I'm the one that's going to slice you up with a kitchen knife, after all.'

'Slice me up?'

'Aw, shush, not literally. Come on, we're here.'

Lucy turns out to be a perfect fountainette, happy to sit still and stare into the distance while I anoint my canvas with her colours. I'd say they are even prettier than mine, although that might be my modesty talking.

'You've got blue blood', I say in awe, painting the azure gaze of a drowning girl.

'Don't be silly', Lucy giggles. 'Why are her eyes so black? It looks like there is nothing inside her.'

TROUBLE

In this barren garden your touch is a chronoscopy.
No need for fading photographs, for half-forgotten melodies
the past sits beside me, strangling me with jealousy
dark green vines grazing my neck, warm fingers
a row of rusted sickles in the sun.
Sweat coats my hair beneath the sky-blue scarf
drips down my old young face. Hand on my cheekbone
a warning. I never knew I could raise my own.
Show me how it was. From the distance
all of it is meaningless. Days with their backs against the stove
dowries of broken lace, songs I sang without my voice.
I am walking through the trees, humming loudly, a song of no name.
I am threading a needle with golden strands,
making a dress fit for an empress.
When my love flows freely it finds many paths
through barren lands. I make a new spring.

THE BEEKEEPER'S DREAM

FADE IN:

EXT. ORCHARD – MORNING

ESTABLISHING SHOT: Snowdrops in the shade of a large tree. It is eerily quiet.

EXT. ORCHARD - AFTERNOON

The weather is grim – rain hammers wooden beehives in a quiet orchard. There are no flowers to be seen, although it is spring.

ASH, a devoted beekeeper, examines the hives while wearing a protective suit. They live alone, usually only talking to their bees. They have a calm and unpretentious presence, content with their chosen profession.

Ash gently lifts the lid on one of the boxes. There are very few live bees crawling on the frame, while a larger number of dead bees lie on the frame and around the box.

Ash brushes a few of the dead bees off the frame. They sprinkle sugar water on the frame before closing the lid of the box. They open the lid of another hive, seeing a similar situation.

CLOSE-UP: their face – brow furrowed in concern. Ash remains standing still in the middle of the hives.

INT. KITCHEN – AFTERNOON

It rains outside. Ash sits at their small kitchen table, a cup of nettle tea in front of them. They listen to a crackling radio which sits on the shelf, its antenna twisted in a 90-degree angle. The radio is surrounded by jars of honey.

NEWSCASTER (O.S.)
(on radio)

The unseasonably cold and wet weather is expected to continue, with cumulative rainfall reaching the annual average total by the end of March in some areas..
(voice crackles, words become unintelligible, then crisp again.)
The ministry of agriculture is estimating that up to two thirds of wheat crops may be lost if the rains continue. In some parts of the country, subzero night temperatures have also caused damage to..

Ash walks over to the radio and flicks the channel selector, switching to a channel playing Dusty Springfield's Windmills of Your Mind: And the world is like an apple whirling silently in space..

EXT. ORCHARD – MORNING

The sun has come out. Ash is kneeling down, inspecting a single blue-bell blooming on the ground. A bee is crawling inside of it. Ash smiles gently, listening to its buzzing.

                                ASH
                            (whispering)

Good morning, my love.. Could you perform a magic trick for me and
                    make these bluebells multiply?

They get up and begin feeding the hives with sugar water. Dark clouds
gather overhead, capturing the bluebell in their shadow.

EXT. ORCHARD – NIGHT

More rain, beating down on the bluebell and running off the hives in
rivulets.

EXT. ORCHARD – MORNING

Grey skies. Ash is in the orchard, inspecting the hives once again, con-
tainer of sweetwater in hand.

The number of live bees has decreased further. There are only a few in-
sects slowly crawling on the frame, while most of it is covered in a layer
of dead bees.

EXT. ORCHARD – SUNSET

It rains. Ash walks into the orchard, humming softly, dressed in white clothes (not the protective suit).

A large fraxinus jaspidea towers over the hives. Ash sits down by the tree, leaning on its trunk. It is very quiet. Ash smooths over their clothes, caresses the surface of the tree, closes their eyes.

DOLLY OUT: Ash drifts to sleep by the tree, in the rain.

EXT. ORCHARD – MORNING

In the morning sunlight, snowdrops bloom in the shade of the tree. A swarm of bees is feeding off them, creating a loud buzzing sound.

FADE TO BLACK.

Kaisa Saarinen grew up in the Finnish countryside and left home as soon as possible. She ended up in London by way of Glasgow, Tokyo, and Oxford. She thinks discretion is hot.

THE FOLLOWING STORIES & POEMS WERE ORIGINALLY PUBLISHED ELSE
WHERE, SOMETIMES IN ALTERED FORMS.

Spectral Anguish in *Anti-Heroin Chic* (February 202

i have no need for a man inside the leather jacket in *Miniskirt* (April 202

Images of Cruelty in *Expat Press* (July 202

Park Hotel in *Sledgehammer Lit* (August 202

Inner Light in *Apocalypse Confidential* (September 202

Exonerate Me in *Zero Readers* (September 202

Hothouse Camellia (for a girl of celluloid) in *Wind-up Mice* (October 20.

There Was a Warning in *Resurrections* (November 202

Reaper in *ffraid* (November 202

Girlhood Sijo in *Babel Tower Noticeboard* (December 202

Uniform of Affection in *The Hungry Ghost Magazine Issue 2* (December 202

Trouble in *Superfroot* (January 202

Published by Feral Dove Books

ISBN 979-8-9856764-2-6

Thank you for being here

Original photographs in this collection were taken by the author, with edits from the publisher

Book design by Evan Femino

feraldove.com

CPSIA information can be obtained
at www.ICGtesting.com
Printed in the USA
LVHW102345200522
719346LV00016B/1596